THE
UNKNOWN MASTERPIECE

From the original French:
La Comédie Humaine: Le Chef-d'œuvre inconnu

By

Honoré De Balzac

The Author of
"Father Goriot"
"Colonel Chabert"
"Sarrasine"

TRANSLATED BY
Katharine Prescott Wormeley

(1831)

ISBN-13: 978-1981508730
ISBN-10: 1981508732

1

CONTENTS

THE UNKNOWN MASTERPIECE

To A LORD

THE
UNKNOWN MASTERPIECE

I.

Gillette

On a cold morning in December, towards the close of the year 1612, a young man, whose clothing betrayed his poverty, was standing before the door of a house in the Rue des Grands-Augustine, in Paris. After walking to and fro for some time with the hesitation of a lover who fears to approach his mistress, however complying she may be, he ended by crossing the threshold and asking if Maitre Francois Porbus were within. At the affirmative answer of an old woman who was sweeping out one of the lower rooms the young man slowly mounted the stairway, stopping from time to time and hesitating, like a newly fledged courier doubtful as to what sort of reception the king might grant him.

When he reached the upper landing of the spiral ascent, he paused a moment before laying hold of a grotesque knocker which ornamented the door of the atelier where the famous painter of Henry IV.—neglected by Marie de Medicis for Rubens—was probably at work. The young man felt the strong sensation which vibrates in the soul of great artists when, in the flush of youth and of their ardor for art, they approach a man of genius or a masterpiece. In all human sentiments there are, as it were, primeval flowers bred of noble enthusiasms, which droop and fade from year to year, till joy is but a memory and glory a lie. Amid such fleeting emotions nothing so resembles love as the young passion of an artist who tastes the first delicious anguish of his destined fame and woe,—a passion daring yet timid, full of vague confidence and sure discouragement. Is there a man, slender in fortune, rich in his spring-time of genius, whose heart has not beaten loudly as he approached a master of his art? If there be, that man will forever lack some heart-string, some touch, I know not what, of his brush, some fibre in his creations, some sentiment in his poetry. When braggarts, self-satisfied and in love with themselves, step early into the fame which belongs rightly to their future achievements, they are men of genius only in the eyes of fools. If talent is to be measured by youthful shyness, by that indefinable modesty which men born to glory lose in the practice of their art, as a pretty woman loses hers among the artifices of coquetry, then this unknown young man might claim to be possessed of genuine merit. The habit of success lessens doubt; and modesty, perhaps, is doubt.

Worn down with poverty and discouragement, and dismayed at this moment by his own presumption, the young neophyte might not have dared to enter the presence of the master to whom we owe our admirable portrait of Henry IV., if chance had not thrown an unexpected assistance in his way. An old man mounted the spiral stairway. The oddity of his dress, the magnificence of his lace ruffles, the solid assurance of his deliberate step, led the youth to assume that this remarkable personage must be the patron, or at least the intimate friend, of the painter. He drew back into a corner of the landing and made room for the new-comer; looking at him attentively and hoping to find either the frank good-nature of the artistic temperament, or the serviceable disposition of those who promote the arts. But on the contrary he fancied he saw something diabolical in the expression of the old man's face,— something, I know not what, which has the quality of alluring the artistic mind.

Imagine a bald head, the brow full and prominent and falling with deep projection over a little flattened nose turned up at the end like the noses of Rabelais and Socrates; a laughing, wrinkled mouth; a short chin boldly chiselled and garnished with a gray beard cut into a point; sea-green eyes, faded perhaps by age, but whose pupils, contrasting with the pearl-white balls on which they floated, cast at times magnetic glances of anger or enthusiasm. The face in other respects was singularly withered and worn by the weariness of old age, and still more, it would seem, by the action of thoughts which had undermined both soul and body. The eyes had lost their lashes, and the eyebrows were scarcely traced along the projecting arches where they belonged. Imagine such a head upon a lean and feeble body, surround it with lace of dazzling whiteness worked in meshes like a fish-slice, festoon the black velvet doublet of the old man with a heavy gold chain, and you will have a faint idea of the exterior of this strange individual, to whose appearance the dusky light of the landing lent fantastic coloring. You might have thought that a canvas of Rembrandt without its frame had walked silently up the stairway, bringing with it the dark atmosphere which was the sign-manual of the great master. The old man cast a look upon the youth which was full of sagacity; then he rapped three times upon the door, and said, when it was opened by a man in feeble health, apparently about forty years of age, "Good-morning, maitre."

Porbus bowed respectfully, and made way for his guest, allowing the youth to pass in at the same time, under the impression that he came with the old man, and taking no further notice of him; all the less perhaps because the neophyte stood still beneath the spell which holds a heaven-born painter as he sees for the first time an atelier filled with the materials and instruments of his art. Daylight came from a casement in the roof and fell, focussed as it were, upon a canvas which rested on an easel in the middle of the room, and which bore, as yet, only three or four chalk lines. The light thus concentrated did not reach the dark angles of the vast atelier; but a few wandering reflections gleamed through the russet shadows on the silvered breastplate of a horseman's cuirass of the fourteenth century as it hung from the wall, or sent sharp lines of light upon the carved and polished cornice of a dresser which held specimens of rare pottery and porcelains, or touched with sparkling points the rough-grained texture of ancient gold-brocaded curtains, flung in broad folds about the room to serve the painter as models for his drapery. Anatomical casts in plaster, fragments and torsos of antique goddesses amorously polished by the kisses of centuries, jostled each other upon shelves and brackets. Innumerable sketches, studies in the three crayons, in ink, and in red chalk covered the walls from floor to ceiling; color-boxes, bottles of oil and turpentine, easels and stools upset or standing at right angles, left but a narrow pathway to the circle of light thrown from the window in the roof, which fell full on the pale face of Porbus and on the ivory skull of his singular visitor.

The attention of the young man was taken exclusively by a picture destined to become famous after those days of tumult and revolution, and which even then was precious in the sight of certain opinionated individuals to whom we owe the preservation of the divine afflatus through the dark days when the life of art was in jeopardy. This noble picture represents the Mary of Egypt as she prepares to pay for her passage by the ship. It is a masterpiece, painted for Marie de Medicis, and afterwards sold by her in the days of her distress.

"I like your saint," said the old man to Porbus, "and I will give you ten golden crowns over and above the queen's offer; but as to entering into competition with her—the devil!"

"You do like her, then?"

"As for that," said the old man, "yes, and no. The good woman is well set-up, but—she is not living. You young men think you have done all when you have drawn the form correctly, and put everything in place according to the laws of anatomy. You color the features with flesh-tones, mixed beforehand on your palette,—taking very good care to shade one side of the face darker than the other; and because you draw now and then from a nude woman standing on a table, you think you can copy nature; you fancy yourselves painters, and imagine that you have got at the secret of God's creations! Pr-r-r-r!—To be a great poet it is not enough to know the rules of syntax and write faultless grammar. Look at your saint, Porbus. At first sight she is admirable; but at the very next glance we perceive that she is glued to the canvas, and that we cannot walk round her. She is a silhouette with only one side, a semblance cut in outline, an image that can't turn nor change her position. I feel no air between this arm and the background of the picture; space and depth are wanting. All is in good perspective; the atmospheric gradations are carefully observed, and yet in spite of your conscientious labor I cannot believe that this beautiful body has the warm breath of life. If I put my hand on that firm, round throat I shall find it cold as marble. No, no, my friend, blood does not run beneath that ivory skin; the purple tide of life does not swell those veins, nor stir those fibres which interlace like net-work below the translucent amber of the brow and breast. This part palpitates with life, but that other part is not living; life and death jostle each other in every detail.

Here, you have a woman; there, a statue; here again, a dead body. Your creation is incomplete. You have breathed only a part of your soul into the well-beloved work. The torch of Prometheus went out in your hands over and over again; there are several parts of your painting on which the celestial flame never shone."

"But why is it so, my dear master?" said Porbus humbly, while the young man could hardly restrain a strong desire to strike the critic.

"Ah! that is the question," said the little old man. "You are floating between two systems,—between drawing and color, between the patient phlegm and honest stiffness of the old Dutch masters and the dazzling warmth and abounding joy of the Italians. You have tried to follow, at one and the same time, Hans Holbein and Titian; Albrecht Durier and Paul Veronese. Well, well! it was a glorious ambition, but what is the result? You have neither the stern attraction of severity nor the deceptive magic of the chiaroscuro. See! at this place the rich, clear color of Titian has forced out the skeleton outline of Albrecht Durier, as molten bronze might burst and overflow a slender mould. Here and there the outline has resisted the flood, and holds back the magnificent torrent of Venetian color. Your figure is neither perfectly well painted nor perfectly well drawn; it bears throughout the signs of this unfortunate indecision. If you did not feel that the fire of your genius was hot enough to weld into one the rival methods, you ought to have chosen honestly the one or the other, and thus attained the unity which conveys one aspect, at least, of life. As it is, you are true only on your middle plane. Your outlines are false; they do not round upon themselves; they suggest nothing behind them. There is truth here," said the old man, pointing to the bosom of the saint; "and here," showing the spot where the shoulder ended against the background; "but there," he added, returning to the throat, "it is all false. Do not inquire into the why and wherefore. I should fill you with despair."

The old man sat down on a stool and held his head in his hands for some minutes in silence.

"Master," said Porbus at length, "I studied that throat from the nude; but, to our sorrow, there are effects in nature which become false or impossible when placed on canvas."

"The mission of art is not to copy nature, but to represent it. You are not an abject copyist, but a poet," cried the old man, hastily interrupting Porbus with a despotic gesture. "If it were not so, a sculptor could reach the height of his art by merely moulding a woman. Try to mould the hand of your mistress, and see what you will get,—ghastly articulations, without the slightest resemblance to her living hand; you must have recourse to the chisel of a man who, without servilely copying that hand, can give it movement and life. It is our mission to seize the mind, soul, countenance of things and beings. Effects! effects! what are they? the mere accidents of the life, and not the life itself. A hand,—since I have taken that as an example,—a hand is not merely a part of the body, it is far more; it expresses and carries on a thought which we must seize and render. Neither the painter nor the poet nor the sculptor should separate the effect from the cause, for they are indissolubly one. The true struggle of art lies there. Many a painter has triumphed through instinct without knowing this theory of art as a theory.

"Yes," continued the old man vehemently, "you draw a woman, but you do not *see* her. That is not the way to force an entrance into the arcana of Nature. Your hand reproduces, without an action of your mind, the model you copied under a master. You do not search out the secrets of form, nor follow its windings and evolutions with enough love and perseverance. Beauty is solemn and severe, and cannot be attained in that way; we must wait and watch its times and seasons, and clasp it firmly ere it yields to us. Form is a Proteus less easily captured, more skilful to double and escape, than the Proteus of fable; it is only at the cost of struggle that we compel it to come forth in its true aspects. You young men are content with the first glimpse you get of it; or, at any rate, with the second or the third. This is not the spirit of the great warriors of art,—invincible powers, not misled by will-o'-the-wisps, but advancing always until they force Nature to lie bare in her divine integrity. That was Raphael's method," said the old man, lifting his velvet cap in homage to the sovereign of art; "his superiority came from the inward essence which seems to break from the inner to the outer of his figures. Form with him was what it is with us,—a medium by which to communicate ideas, sensations, feelings; in short, the infinite poesy of being. Every figure is a world; a portrait, whose original stands forth like a sublime vision, colored with the rainbow tints of light, drawn by the monitions of an inward voice, laid bare by a divine finger which points to the past of its whole existence as the source of its given expression. You clothe your women with delicate skins and glorious draperies of hair, but where is the blood which begets the passion or the peace of their souls, and is the cause of what you call 'effects'? Your saint is a dark woman; but this, my poor Porbus, belongs to a fair one. Your figures are pale, colored phantoms, which you present to our eyes; and you call that painting! art! Because you make something which looks more like a woman than a house, you think you have touched the goal; proud of not being obliged to write "currus venustus" or "pulcher homo" on the frame of your picture, you think yourselves majestic artists like our great forefathers. Ha, ha! you have not got there yet, my little men; you will use up many a crayon and spoil many a canvas before you reach that height. Undoubtedly a woman carries her head this way and her petticoats that way; her eyes soften and droop with just that look of resigned gentleness; the throbbing shadow of the eyelashes falls exactly thus upon her cheek. That is it, and—that is *not it.* What lacks? A mere nothing; but that mere nothing is *all.* You have given the shadow of life, but you have not given its fulness, its being, its—I know not what—soul, perhaps, which floats vaporously about the tabernacle of flesh; in short, that flower of life which Raphael and Titian culled. Start from the point you have now attained, and perhaps you may yet paint a worthy picture; you grew weary too soon. Mediocrity will extol your work; but the true artist smiles. O Mabuse! O my master!" added this singular person, "you were a thief; you have robbed us of your life, your knowledge, your art! But at least," he resumed after a pause, "this picture is better than the paintings of that rascally Rubens, with his mountains of Flemish flesh daubed with vermilion, his cascades of red hair, and his hurly-burly of color. At any rate, you have got the elements of color, drawing, and sentiment,—the three essential parts of art."

"But the saint is sublime, good sir!" cried the young man in a loud voice, waking from a deep reverie. "These figures, the saint and the boatman, have a subtile meaning which the Italian painters cannot give. I do not know one of them who could have invented that hesitation of the boatman."

"Does the young fellow belong to you?" asked Porbus of the old man.

"Alas, maitre, forgive my boldness," said the neophyte, blushing. "I am all unknown; only a dauber by instinct. I have just come to Paris, that fountain of art and science."

"Let us see what you can do," said Porbus, giving him a red crayon and a piece of paper.

The unknown copied the saint with an easy turn of his hand.

"Oh! oh!" exclaimed the old man, "what is your name?"

The youth signed the drawing: Nicolas Poussin.

"Not bad for a beginner," said the strange being who had discoursed so wildly. "I see that it is worth while to talk art before you. I don't blame you for admiring Porbus's saint. It is a masterpiece for the world at large; only those who are behind the veil of the holy of holies can perceive its errors. But you are worthy of a lesson, and capable of understanding it. I will show you how little is needed to turn that picture into a true masterpiece. Give all your eyes and all your attention; such a chance of instruction may never fall in your way again. Your palette, Porbus."

Porbus fetched his palette and brushes. The little old man turned up his cuffs with convulsive haste, slipped his thumb through the palette charged with prismatic colors, and snatched, rather than took, the handful of brushes which Porbus held out to him. As he did so his beard, cut to a point, seemed to quiver with the eagerness of an incontinent fancy; and while he filled his brush he muttered between his teeth:—

"Colors fit to fling out of the window with the man who ground them,— crude, false, revolting! who can paint with them?"

Then he dipped the point of his brush with feverish haste into the various tints, running through the whole scale with more rapidity than the organist of a cathedral runs up the gamut of the "O Filii" at Easter.

Porbus and Poussin stood motionless on either side of the easel, plunged in passionate contemplation.

"See, young man," said the old man without turning round, "see how with three or four touches and a faint bluish glaze you can make the air circulate round the head of the poor saint, who was suffocating in that thick atmosphere. Look how the drapery now floats, and you see that the breeze lifts it; just now it looked like heavy linen held out by pins. Observe that the satiny lustre I am putting on the bosom gives it the plump suppleness of the flesh of a young girl. See how this tone of mingled reddish-brown and ochre warms up the cold grayness of that large shadow where the blood seemed to stagnate rather than flow. Young man, young man! what I am showing you now no other master in the world can teach you. Mabuse alone knew the secret of giving life to form. Mabuse had but one pupil, and I am he. I never took a pupil, and I am an old man now. You are intelligent enough to guess at what should follow from the little that I shall show you to-day."

While he was speaking, the extraordinary old man was giving touches here and there to all parts of the picture. Here two strokes of the brush, there one, but each so telling that together they brought out a new painting,—a painting steeped, as it were, in light. He worked with such passionate ardor that the sweat rolled in great drops from his bald brow; and his motions seemed to be jerked out of him with such rapidity and impatience that the young Poussin fancied a demon, encased with the body of this singular being, was working his hands fantastically like those of a puppet without, or even against, the will of their owner. The unnatural brightness of his eyes, the convulsive movements which seemed the result of some mental resistance, gave to this fancy of the youth a semblance of truth which reacted upon his lively imagination. The old man worked on, muttering half to himself, half to his neophyte:—

"Paf! paf! paf! that is how we butter it on, young man. Ah! my little pats, you are right; warm up that icy tone. Come, come!—pon, pon, pon,—" he continued, touching up the spots where he had complained of a lack of life, hiding under layers of color the conflicting methods, and regaining the unity of tone essential to an ardent Egyptian.

"Now see, my little friend, it is only the last touches of the brush that count for anything. Porbus put on a hundred; I have only put on one or two. Nobody will thank us for what is underneath, remember that!"

At last the demon paused; the old man turned to Porbus and Poussin, who stood mute with admiration, and said to them,—

"It is not yet equal to my Beautiful Nut-girl; still, one can put one's name to such a work. Yes, I will sign it," he added, rising to fetch a mirror in which to look at what he had done. "Now let us go and breakfast. Come, both of you, to my house. I have some smoked ham and good wine. Hey! hey! in spite of the degenerate times we will talk painting; we are strong ourselves. Here is a little man," he continued, striking Nicolas Poussin on the shoulder, "who has the faculty."

Observing the shabby cap of the youth, he pulled from his belt a leathern purse from which he took two gold pieces and offered them to him, saying,—

"I buy your drawing."

"Take them," said Porbus to Poussin, seeing that the latter trembled and blushed with shame, for the young scholar had the pride of poverty; "take them, he has the ransom of two kings in his pouch."

The three left the atelier and proceeded, talking all the way of art, to a handsome wooden house standing near the Pont Saint-Michel, whose window-casings and arabesque decoration amazed Poussin. The embryo painter soon found himself in one of the rooms on the ground floor seated, beside a good fire, at a table covered with appetizing dishes, and, by unexpected good fortune, in company with two great artists who treated him with kindly attention.

"Young man," said Porbus, observing that he was speechless, with his eyes fixed on a picture, "do not look at that too long, or you will fall into despair."

It was the Adam of Mabuse, painted by that wayward genius to enable him to get out of the prison where his creditors had kept him so long. The figure presented such fulness and force of reality that Nicolas Poussin began to comprehend the meaning of the bewildering talk of the old man. The latter looked at the picture with a satisfied but not enthusiastic manner, which seemed to say, "I have done better myself."

"There is life in the form," he remarked. "My poor master surpassed himself there; but observe the want of truth in the background. The man is living, certainly; he rises and is coming towards us; but the atmosphere, the sky, the air that we breathe, see, feel,—where are they? Besides, that is only a man; and the being who came first from the hand of God must needs have had something divine about him which is lacking here. Mabuse said so himself with vexation in his sober moments."

Poussin looked alternately at the old man and at Porbus with uneasy curiosity. He turned to the latter as if to ask the name of their host, but the painter laid a finger on his lips with an air of mystery, and the young man, keenly interested, kept silence, hoping that sooner or later some word of the conversation might enable him to guess the name of the old man, whose wealth and genius were sufficiently attested by the respect which Porbus showed him, and by the marvels of art heaped together in the picturesque apartment.

Poussin, observing against the dark panelling of the wall a magnificent portrait of a woman, exclaimed aloud, "What a magnificent Giorgione!"

"No," remarked the old man, "that is only one of my early daubs."

"Zounds!" cried Poussin naively; "are you the king of painters?"

The old man smiled, as if long accustomed to such homage. "Maitre Frenhofer," said Porbus, "could you order up a little of your good Rhine wine for me?"

"Two casks," answered the host; "one to pay for the pleasure of looking at your pretty sinner this morning, and the other as a mark of friendship."

"Ah! if I were not so feeble," resumed Porbus, "and if you would consent to let me see your Beautiful Nut-girl, I too could paint some lofty picture, grand and yet profound, where the forms should have the living life."

"Show my work!" exclaimed the old man, with deep emotion. "No, no! I have still to bring it to perfection. Yesterday, towards evening, I thought it was finished. Her eyes were liquid, her flesh trembled, her tresses waved—she breathed! And yet, though I have grasped the secret of rendering on a flat canvas the relief and roundness of nature, this morning at dawn I saw many errors. Ah! to attain that glorious result, I have studied to their depths the masters of color. I have analyzed and lifted, layer by layer, the colors of Titian, king of light. Like him, great sovereign of art, I have sketched my figure in light clear tones of supple yet solid color; for shadow is but an accident,—remember that, young man. Then I worked backward, as it were; and by means of half-tints, and glazings whose transparency I kept diminishing little by little, I was able to cast strong shadows deepening almost to blackness. The shadows of ordinary painters are not of the same texture as their tones of light. They are wood, brass, iron, anything you please except flesh in shadow. We feel that if the figures changed position the shady places would not be wiped off, and would remain dark spots which never could be made luminous. I have avoided that blunder, though many of our most illustrious painters have fallen into it. In my work you will see whiteness beneath the opacity of the broadest shadow. Unlike the crowd of ignoramuses, who fancy they draw correctly because they can paint one good vanishing line, I have not dryly outlined my figures, nor brought out superstitiously minute anatomical details; for, let me tell you, the human body does not end off with a line. In that respect sculptors get nearer to the truth of nature than we do. Nature is all curves, each wrapping or overlapping another. To speak rigorously, there is no such thing as drawing. Do not laugh, young man; no matter how strange that saying seems to you, you will understand the reasons for it one of these days. A line is a means by which man explains to himself the effect of light upon a given object; but there is no such thing as a line in nature, where all things are rounded and full. It is only in modelling that we really draw,—in other words, that we detach things from their surroundings and put them in their due relief. The proper distribution of light can alone reveal the whole body. For this reason I do not sharply define lineaments; I diffuse about their outline a haze of warm, light half-tints, so that I defy any one to place a finger on the exact spot where the parts join the groundwork of the picture. If seen near by this sort of work has a woolly effect, and is wanting in nicety and precision; but go a few steps off and the parts fall into place; they take their proper form and detach themselves,—the body turns, the limbs stand out, we feel the air circulating around them.

"Nevertheless," he continued, sadly, "I am not satisfied; there are moments when I have my doubts. Perhaps it would be better not to sketch a single line. I ask myself if I ought not to grasp the figure first by its highest lights, and then work down to the darker portions. Is not that the method of the sun, divine painter of the universe? O Nature, Nature! who has ever caught thee in thy flights? Alas! the heights of knowledge, like the depths of ignorance, lead to unbelief. I doubt my work."

The old man paused, then resumed. "For ten years I have worked, young man; but what are ten short years in the long struggle with Nature? We do not know the type it cost Pygmalion to make the only statue that ever walked—"

He fell into a reverie and remained, with fixed eyes, oblivious of all about him, playing mechanically with his knife.

"See, he is talking to his own soul," said Porbus in a low voice.

The words acted like a spell on Nicolas Poussin, filling him with the inexplicable curiosity of a true artist. The strange old man, with his white eyes fixed in stupor, became to the wondering youth something more than a man; he seemed a fantastic spirit inhabiting an unknown sphere, and waking by its touch confused ideas within the soul. We can no more define the moral phenomena of this species of fascination than we can render in words the emotions excited in the heart of an exile by a song which recalls his fatherland. The contempt which the old man affected to pour upon the noblest efforts of art, his wealth, his manners, the respectful deference shown to him by Porbus, his work guarded so secretly,—a work of patient toil, a work no doubt of genius, judging by the head of the Virgin which Poussin had so naively admired, and which, beautiful beside even the Adam of Mabuse, betrayed the imperial touch of a great artist,—in short, everything about the strange old man seemed beyond the limits of human nature. The rich imagination of the youth fastened upon the one perceptible and clear clew to the mystery of this supernatural being,—the presence of the artistic nature, that wild impassioned nature to which such mighty powers have been confided, which too often abuses those powers, and drags cold reason and common souls, and even lovers of art, over stony and arid places, where for such there is neither pleasure nor instruction; while to the artistic soul itself,— that white-winged angel of sportive fancy,—epics, works of art, and visions rise along the way. It is a nature, an essence, mocking yet kind, fruitful though destitute. Thus, for the enthusiastic Poussin, the old man became by sudden transfiguration Art itself,—art with all its secrets, its transports, and its dreams.

"Yes, my dear Porbus," said Frenhofer, speaking half in reverie, "I have never yet beheld a perfect woman; a body whose outlines were faultless and whose flesh-tints—Ah! where lives she?" he cried, interrupting his own words; "where lives the lost Venus of the ancients, so long sought for, whose scattered beauty we snatch by glimpses? Oh! to see for a moment, a single moment, the divine completed nature,—the ideal,—I would give my all of fortune. Yes; I would search thee out, celestial Beauty! in thy farthest sphere. Like Orpheus, I would go down to hell to win back the life of art—"

"Let us go," said Porbus to Poussin; "he neither sees nor hears us any longer."

"Let us go to his atelier," said the wonder-struck young man.

"Oh! the old dragon has guarded the entrance. His treasure is out of our reach. I have not waited for your wish or urging to attempt an assault on the mystery."

"Mystery! then there is a mystery?"

"Yes," answered Porbus. "Frenhofer was the only pupil Mabuse was willing to teach. He became the friend, saviour, father of that unhappy man, and he sacrificed the greater part of his wealth to satisfy the mad passions of his master. In return, Mabuse bequeathed to him the secret of relief, the power of giving life to form,—that flower of nature, our perpetual despair, which Mabuse had seized so well that once, having sold and drunk the value of a flowered damask which he should have worn at the entrance of Charles V., he made his appearance in a paper garment painted to resemble damask. The splendor of the stuff attracted the attention of the emperor, who, wishing to compliment the old drunkard, laid a hand upon his shoulder and discovered the deception. Frenhofer is a man carried away by the passion of his art; he sees above and beyond what other painters see. He has meditated deeply on color and the absolute truth of lines; but by dint of much research, much thought, much study, he has come to doubt the object for which he is searching. In his hours of despair he fancies that drawing does not exist, and that lines can render nothing but geometric figures. That, of course, is not true; because with a black line which has no color we can represent the human form. This proves that our art is made up, like nature, of an infinite number of elements. Drawing gives the skeleton, and color gives the life; but life without the skeleton is a far more incomplete thing than the skeleton without the life. But there is a higher truth still,—namely, that practice and observation are the essentials of a painter; and that if reason and poesy persist in wrangling with the tools, the brushes, we shall be brought to doubt, like Frenhofer, who is as much excited in brain as he is exalted in art. A sublime painter, indeed; but he had the misfortune to be born rich, and that enables him to stray into theory and conjecture. Do not imitate him. Work! work! painters should theorize with their brushes in their hands."

"We will contrive to get in," cried Poussin, not listening to Porbus, and thinking only of the hidden masterpiece.

Porbus smiled at the youth's enthusiasm, and bade him farewell with a kindly invitation to come and visit him.

Nicolas Poussin returned slowly towards the Rue de la Harpe and passed, without observing that he did so, the modest hostelry where he was lodging. Returning presently upon his steps, he ran up the miserable stairway with anxious rapidity until he reached an upper chamber nestling between the joists of a roof "en colombage,"—the plain, slight covering of the houses of old Paris. Near the single and gloomy window of the room sat a young girl, who rose quickly as the door opened, with a gesture of love; she had recognized the young man's touch upon the latch.

"What is the matter?" she asked.

"It is—it is," he cried, choking with joy, "that I feel myself a painter! I have doubted it till now; but to-day I believe in myself. I can be a great man. Ah, Gillette, we shall be rich, happy! There is gold in these brushes!"

Suddenly he became silent. His grave and earnest face lost its expression of joy; he was comparing the immensity of his hopes with the mediocrity of his means. The walls of the garret were covered with bits of paper on which were crayon sketches; he possessed only four clean canvases. Colors were at that time costly, and the poor gentleman gazed at a palette that was well-nigh bare. In the midst of this poverty he felt within himself an indescribable wealth of heart and the superabundant force of consuming genius. Brought to Paris by a gentleman of his acquaintance, and perhaps by the monition of his own talent, he had suddenly found a mistress,—one of those generous and noble souls who are ready to suffer by the side of a great man; espousing his poverty, studying to comprehend his caprices, strong to bear deprivation and bestow love, as others are daring in the display of luxury and in parading the insensibility of their hearts. The smile which flickered on her lips brightened as with gold the darkness of the garret and rivalled the effulgence of the skies; for the sun did not always shine in the heavens, but she was always here,— calm and collected in her passion, living in his happiness, his griefs; sustaining the genius which overflowed in love ere it found in art its destined expression.

"Listen, Gillette; come!"

The obedient, happy girl sprang lightly on the painter's knee. She was all grace and beauty, pretty as the spring-time, decked with the wealth of feminine charm, and lighting all with the fire of a noble soul.

"O God!" he exclaimed, "I can never tell her!"

"A secret!" she cried; "then I must know it."

Poussin was lost in thought.

"Tell me."

"Gillette, poor, beloved heart!"

"Ah! do you want something of me?"

"Yes."

"If you want me to pose as I did the other day," she said, with a little pouting air, "I will not do it. Your eyes say nothing to me, then. You look at me, but you do not think of me."

"Would you like me to copy another woman?"

"Perhaps," she answered, "if she were very ugly."

"Well," continued Poussin, in a grave tone, "if to make me a great painter it were necessary to pose to some one else—"

"You are testing me," she interrupted; "you know well that I would not do it."

Poussin bent his head upon his breast like a man succumbing to joy or grief too great for his spirit to bear.

"Listen," she said, pulling him by the sleeve of his worn doublet, "I told you, Nick, that I would give my life for you; but I never said—never!—that I, a living woman, would renounce my love."

"Renounce it?" cried Poussin.

"If I showed myself thus to another you would love me no longer; and I myself, I should feel unworthy of your love. To obey your caprices, ah, that is simple and natural! in spite of myself, I am proud and happy in doing thy dear will; but to another, fy!"

"Forgive me, my own Gillette," said the painter, throwing himself at her feet. "I would rather be loved than famous. To me thou art more precious than fortune and honors. Yes, away with these brushes! burn those sketches! I have been mistaken. My vocation is to love thee,—thee alone! I am not a painter, I am thy lover. Perish art and all its secrets!"

She looked at him admiringly, happy and captivated by his passion. She reigned; she felt instinctively that the arts were forgotten for her sake, and flung at her feet like grains of incense.

"Yet he is only an old man," resumed Poussin. "In you he would see only a woman. You are the perfect woman whom he seeks."

"Love should grant all things!" she exclaimed, ready to sacrifice love's scruples to reward the lover who thus seemed to sacrifice his art to her. "And yet," she added, "it would be my ruin. Ah, to suffer for thy good! Yes, it is glorious! But thou wilt forget me. How came this cruel thought into thy mind?"

"It came there, and yet I love thee," he said, with a sort of contrition. "Am I, then, a wretch?"

"Let us consult Pere Hardouin."

"No, no! it must be a secret between us."

"Well, I will go; but thou must not be present," she said. "Stay at the door, armed with thy dagger. If I cry out, enter and kill the man."

Forgetting all but his art, Poussin clasped her in his arms.

"He loves me no longer!" thought Gillette, when she was once more alone.

She regretted her promise. But before long she fell a prey to an anguish far more cruel than her regret; and she struggled vainly to drive forth a terrible fear which forced its way into her mind. She felt that she loved him less as the suspicion rose in her heart that he was less worthy than she had thought him.

II.

Catherine Lescault

Three months after the first meeting of Porbus and Poussin, the former went to see Maitre Frenhofer. He found the old man a prey to one of those deep, self-developed discouragements, whose cause, if we are to believe the mathematicians of health, lies in a bad digestion, in the wind, in the weather, in some swelling of the intestines, or else, according to casuists, in the imperfections of our moral nature; the fact being that the good man was simply worn out by the effort to complete his mysterious picture. He was seated languidly in a large oaken chair of vast dimensions covered with black leather; and without changing his melancholy attitude he cast on Porbus the distant glance of a man sunk in absolute dejection.

"Well, maitre," said Porbus, "was the distant ultra-marine, for which you journeyed to Brussels, worthless? Are you unable to grind a new white? Is the oil bad, or the brushes restive?"

"Alas!" cried the old man, "I thought for one moment that my work was accomplished; but I must have deceived myself in some of the details. I shall have no peace until I clear up my doubts. I am about to travel; I go to Turkey, Asia, Greece, in search of models. I must compare my picture with various types of Nature. It may be that I have up *there*," he added, letting a smile of satisfaction flicker on his lip, "Nature herself. At times I am half afraid that a brush may wake this woman, and that she will disappear from sight."

He rose suddenly, as if to depart at once. "Wait," exclaimed Porbus. "I have come in time to spare you the costs and fatigues of such a journey."

"How so?" asked Frenhofer, surprised.

"Young Poussin is beloved by a woman whose incomparable beauty is without imperfection. But, my dear master, if he consents to lend her to you, at least you must let us see your picture."

The old man remained standing, motionless, in a state bordering on stupefaction. "What!" he at last exclaimed, mournfully. "Show my creature, my spouse?—tear off the veil with which I have chastely hidden my joy? It would be prostitution! For ten years I have lived with this woman; she is mine, mine alone! she loves me! Has she not smiled upon me as, touch by touch, I painted her? She has a soul,—the soul with which I endowed her. She would blush if other eyes than mine beheld her. Let her be seen?—where is the husband, the lover, so debased as to lend his wife to dishonor? When you paint a picture for the court you do not put your whole soul into it; you sell to courtiers your tricked-out lay-figures. My painting is not a picture; it is a sentiment, a passion! Born in my atelier, she must remain a virgin there. She shall not leave it unclothed. Poesy and women give themselves bare, like truth, to lovers only. Have we the model of Raphael, the Angelica of Ariosto, the Beatrice of Dante? No, we see but their semblance. Well, the work which I keep hidden behind bolts and bars is an exception to all other art. It is not a canvas; it is a woman,—a woman with whom I weep and laugh and think and talk. Would you have me resign the joy of ten years, as I might throw away a worn-out doublet? Shall I, in a moment, cease to be father, lover, creator?—this woman is not a creature; she is my creation. Bring your young man; I will give him my treasures,—paintings of Correggio, Michael-Angelo, Titian; I will kiss the print of his feet in the dust,—but make him my rival? Shame upon me! Ha! I am more a lover than I am a painter. I shall have the strength to burn my Nut-girl ere I render my last sigh; but suffer her to endure the glance of a man, a young man, a painter?—No, no! I would kill on the morrow the man who polluted her with a look! I would kill you,—you, my friend,—if you did not worship her on your knees; and think you I would submit my idol to the cold eyes and stupid criticisms of fools? Ah, love is a mystery! its life is in the depths of the soul; it dies when a man says, even to his friend, Here is she whom I love."

The old man seemed to renew his youth; his eyes had the brilliancy and fire of life, his pale cheeks blushed a vivid red, his hands trembled. Porbus, amazed by the passionate violence with which he uttered these words, knew not how to answer a feeling so novel and yet so profound. Was the old man under the thraldom of an artist's fancy? Or did these ideas flow from the unspeakable fanaticism produced at times in every mind by the long gestation of a noble work? Was it possible to bargain with this strange and whimsical being?

Filled with such thoughts, Porbus said to the old man, "Is it not woman for woman? Poussin lends his mistress to your eyes."

"What sort of mistress is that?" cried Frenhofer. "She will betray him sooner or later. Mine will be to me forever faithful."

"Well," returned Porbus, "then let us say no more. But before you find, even in Asia, a woman as beautiful, as perfect, as the one I speak of, you may be dead, and your picture forever unfinished."

"Oh, it is finished!" said Frenhofer. "Whoever sees it will find a woman lying on a velvet bed, beneath curtains; perfumes are exhaling from a golden tripod by her side: he will be tempted to take the tassels of the cord that holds back the curtain; he will think he sees the bosom of Catherine Lescaut,—a model called the Beautiful Nut-girl; he will see it rise and fall with the movement of her breathing. Yet—I wish I could be sure—"

"Go to Asia, then," said Porbus hastily, fancying he saw some hesitation in the old man's eye.

Porbus made a few steps towards the door of the room. At this moment Gillette and Nicolas Poussin reached the entrance of the house. As the young girl was about to enter, she dropped the arm of her lover and shrank back as if overcome by a presentiment. "What am I doing here?" she said to Poussin, in a deep voice, looking at him fixedly.

"Gillette, I leave you mistress of your actions; I will obey your will. You are my conscience, my glory. Come home; I shall be happy, perhaps, if you, yourself—"

"Have I a self when you speak thus to me? Oh, no! I am but a child. Come," she continued, seeming to make a violent effort. "If our love perishes, if I put into my heart a long regret, thy fame shall be the guerdon of my obedience to thy will. Let us enter. I may yet live again,—a memory on thy palette."

Opening the door of the house the two lovers met Porbus coming out. Astonished at the beauty of the young girl, whose eyes were still wet with tears, he caught her all trembling by the hand and led her to the old master.

"There!" he cried; "is she not worth all the masterpieces in the world?"

Frenhofer quivered. Gillette stood before him in the ingenuous, simple attitude of a young Georgian, innocent and timid, captured by brigands and offered to a slave-merchant. A modest blush suffused her cheeks, her eyes were lowered, her hands hung at her sides, strength seemed to abandon her, and her tears protested against the violence done to her purity. Poussin cursed himself, and repented of his folly in bringing this treasure from their peaceful garret. Once more he became a lover rather than an artist; scruples convulsed his heart as he saw the eye of the old painter regain its youth and, with the artist's habit, disrobe as it were the beauteous form of the young girl. He was seized with the jealous frenzy of a true lover.

"Gillette!" he cried; "let us go."

At this cry, with its accent of love, his mistress raised her eyes joyfully and looked at him; then she ran into his arms.

"Ah! you love me still?" she whispered, bursting into tears.

Though she had had strength to hide her suffering, she had none to hide her joy.

"Let me have her for one moment," exclaimed the old master, "and you shall compare her with my Catherine. Yes, yes; I consent!"

There was love in the cry of Frenhofer as in that of Poussin, mingled with jealous coquetry on behalf of his semblance of a woman; he seemed to revel in the triumph which the beauty of his virgin was about to win over the beauty of the living woman.

"Do not let him retract," cried Porbus, striking Poussin on the shoulder. "The fruits of love wither in a day; those of art are immortal."

"Can it be," said Gillette, looking steadily at Poussin and at Porbus, "that I am nothing more than a woman to him?"

She raised her head proudly; and as she glanced at Frenhofer with flashing eyes she saw her lover gazing once more at the picture he had formerly taken for a Giorgione.

"Ah!" she cried, "let us go in; he never looked at me like that!"

"Old man!" said Poussin, roused from his meditation by Gillette's voice, "see this sword. I will plunge it into your heart at the first cry of that young girl. I will set fire to your house, and no one shall escape from it. Do you understand me?"

His look was gloomy and the tones of his voice were terrible. His attitude, and above all the gesture with which he laid his hand upon the weapon, comforted the poor girl, who half forgave him for thus sacrificing her to his art and to his hopes of a glorious future.

Porbus and Poussin remained outside the closed door of the atelier, looking at one another in silence. At first the painter of the Egyptian Mary uttered a few exclamations: "Ah, she unclothes herself!"—"He tells her to stand in the light!"—"He compares them!" but he grew silent as he watched the mournful face of the young man; for though old painters have none of such petty scruples in presence of their art, yet they admire them in others, when they are fresh and pleasing. The young man held his hand on his sword, and his ear seemed glued to the panel of the door. Both men, standing darkly in the shadow, looked like conspirators waiting the hour to strike a tyrant.

"Come in! come in!" cried the old man, beaming with happiness. "My work is perfect; I can show it now with pride. Never shall painter, brushes, colors, canvas, light, produce the rival of Catherine Lescaut, the Beautiful Nut-girl."

Porbus and Poussin, seized with wild curiosity, rushed into the middle of a vast atelier filled with dust, where everything lay in disorder, and where they saw a few paintings hanging here and there upon the walls. They stopped before the figure of a woman, life-sized and half nude, which filled them with eager admiration.

"Do not look at that," said Frenhofer, "it is only a daub which I made to study a pose; it is worth nothing. Those are my errors," he added, waving his hand towards the enchanting compositions on the walls around them.

At these words Porbus and Poussin, amazed at the disdain which the master showed for such marvels of art, looked about them for the secret treasure, but could see it nowhere.

"There it is!" said the old man, whose hair fell in disorder about his face, which was scarlet with supernatural excitement. His eyes sparkled, and his breast heaved like that of a young man beside himself with love.

"Ah!" he cried, "did you not expect such perfection? You stand before a woman, and you are looking for a picture! There are such depths on that canvas, the air within it is so true, that you are unable to distinguish it from the air you breathe. Where is art? Departed, vanished! Here is the form itself of a young girl. Have I not caught the color, the very life of the line which seems to terminate the body? The same phenomenon which we notice around fishes in the water is also about objects which float in air. See how these outlines spring forth from the background. Do you not feel that you could pass your hand behind those shoulders? For seven years have I studied these effects of light coupled with form. That hair,—is it not bathed in light? Why, she breathes! That bosom,—see! Ah! who would not worship it on bended knee? The flesh palpitates! Wait, she is about to rise; wait!"

"Can you see anything?" whispered Poussin to Porbus.

"Nothing. Can you?"

"No."

The two painters drew back, leaving the old man absorbed in ecstasy, and tried to see if the light, falling plumb upon the canvas at which he pointed, had neutralized all effects. They examined the picture, moving from right to left, standing directly before it, bending, swaying, rising by turns.

"Yes, yes; it is really a canvas," cried Frenhofer, mistaking the purpose of their examination. "See, here is the frame, the easel; these are my colors, my brushes." And he caught up a brush which he held out to them with a naive motion.

"The old rogue is making game of us," said Poussin, coming close to the pretended picture. "I can see nothing here but a mass of confused color, crossed by a multitude of eccentric lines, making a sort of painted wall."

"We are mistaken. See!" returned Porbus.

Coming nearer, they perceived in a corner of the canvas the point of a naked foot, which came forth from the chaos of colors, tones, shadows hazy and undefined, misty and without form,—an enchanting foot, a living foot. They stood lost in admiration before this glorious fragment breaking forth from the incredible, slow, progressive destruction around it. The foot seemed to them like the torso of some Grecian Venus, brought to light amid the ruins of a burned city.

"There is a woman beneath it all!" cried Porbus, calling Poussin's attention to the layers of color which the old painter had successively laid on, believing that he thus brought his work to perfection. The two men turned towards him with one accord, beginning to comprehend, though vaguely, the ecstasy in which he lived.

"He means it in good faith," said Porbus.

"Yes, my friend," answered the old man, rousing from his abstraction, "we need faith; faith in art. We must live with our work for years before we can produce a creation like that. Some of these shadows have cost me endless toil. See, there on her cheek, below the eyes, a faint half-shadow; if you observed it in Nature you might think it could hardly be rendered. Well, believe me, I took unheard-of pains to reproduce that effect. My dear Porbus, look attentively at my work, and you will comprehend what I have told you about the manner of treating form and outline. Look at the light on the bosom, and see how by a series of touches and higher lights firmly laid on I have managed to grasp light itself, and combine it with the dazzling whiteness of the clearer tones; and then see how, by an opposite method,—smoothing off the sharp contrasts and the texture of the color,—I have been able, by caressing the outline of my figure and veiling it with cloudy half-tints, to do away with the very idea of drawing and all other artificial means, and give to the form the aspect and roundness of Nature itself. Come nearer, and you will see the work more distinctly; if too far off it disappears. See! there, at that point, it is, I think, most remarkable." And with the end of his brush he pointed to a spot of clear light color.

Porbus struck the old man on the shoulder, turning to Poussin as he did so, and said, "Do you know that he is one of our greatest painters?"

"He is a poet even more than he is a painter," answered Poussin gravely.

"There," returned Porbus, touching the canvas, "is the ultimate end of our art on earth."

"And from thence," added Poussin, "it rises, to enter heaven."

"How much happiness is there!—upon that canvas," said Porbus.

The absorbed old man gave no heed to their words; he was smiling at his visionary woman.

"But sooner or later, he will perceive that there is nothing there," cried Poussin.

"Nothing there!—upon my canvas?" said Frenhofer, looking first at the two painters, and then at his imaginary picture.

"What have you done?" cried Porbus, addressing Poussin.

The old man seized the arm of the young man violently, and said to him, "You see nothing?—clown, infidel, scoundrel, dolt! Why did you come here? My good Porbus," he added, turning to his friend, "is it possible that you, too, are jesting with me? Answer; I am your friend. Tell me, can it be that I have spoiled my picture?"

Porbus hesitated, and feared to speak; but the anxiety painted on the white face of the old man was so cruel that he was constrained to point to the canvas and utter the word, "See!"

Frenhofer looked at his picture for a space of a moment, and staggered.

"Nothing! nothing! after toiling ten years!"

He sat down and wept.

"Am I then a fool, an idiot? Have I neither talent nor capacity? Am I no better than a rich man who walks, and can only walk? Have I indeed produced nothing?"

He gazed at the canvas through tears. Suddenly he raised himself proudly and flung a lightning glance upon the two painters.

"By the blood, by the body, by the head of Christ, you are envious men who seek to make me think she is spoiled, that you may steal her from me. I—I see her!" he cried. "She is wondrously beautiful!"

At this moment Poussin heard the weeping of Gillette as she stood, forgotten, in a corner.

"What troubles thee, my darling?" asked the painter, becoming once more a lover.

"Kill me!" she answered. "I should be infamous if I still loved thee, for I despise thee. I admire thee; but thou hast filled me with horror. I love, and yet already I hate thee."

While Poussin listened to Gillette, Frenhofer drew a green curtain before his Catherine, with the grave composure of a jeweller locking his drawers when he thinks that thieves are near him. He cast at the two painters a look which was profoundly dissimulating, full of contempt and suspicion; then, with convulsive haste, he silently pushed them through the door of his atelier. When they reached the threshold of his house he said to them, "Adieu, my little friends."

The tone of this farewell chilled the two painters with fear.

On the morrow Porbus, alarmed, went again to visit Frenhofer, and found that he had died during the night, after having burned his paintings.

THE END